A MPONGWE TALE

Princess Gorilla
and a New Kind of Water

retold by VERNA AARDEMA
pictures by VICTORIA CHESS

DIAL BOOKS FOR YOUNG READERS ◆ New York

Published by Dial Books for Young Readers
A Division of Penguin Books USA Inc.
375 Hudson Street ◆ New York, New York 10014

Library of Congress Catalog Card Number: 86-32888
Printed in Hong Kong by South China Printing Company (1988) Limited
First Pied Piper Printing 1991
E
1   3   5   7   9   10   8   6   4   2

A Pied Piper Book is a registered trademark of
Dial Books for Young Readers,
a division of Penguin Books USA Inc.,
® TM 1,163,686 and ® TM 1,054,312.

PRINCESS GORILLA AND A NEW KIND OF WATER
is published in a hardcover edition by
Dial Books for Young Readers.
ISBN 0-8037-0914-5

The full-color artwork was prepared using pen and inks,
dyes, and colored pencils. It was then color-separated and
reproduced as red, blue, yellow, and black halftones.

To our little "princess,"
Lauren Marie Aardema
V.A.

For Charlie and Alexandra
V.C.

In a jungle in Africa there once lived a gorilla king who had a beautiful daughter. When she was of marriageable age, he said to her, "My daughter, I'm going to find you a husband who is very strong and brave."

"But, Father," protested Princess Gorilla, "I just want to marry someone who loves me!" And she thought of the handsome young male gorilla who sometimes played tag with her in the wawa trees.

However, King Gorilla thought he knew best. And he pondered over what sort of test he might use to prove a man strong enough and brave enough to be his son-in-law.

One day at the edge of a road King Gorilla found a barrel that had fallen off a trader's wagon. The word VINEGAR was painted on it. But King Gorilla could not read, so he did not know what was inside. He rolled the heavy barrel back to his village.

Then he pulled out the bung near the bottom of the barrel.
Something that looked like water squirted out. He quickly re-
placed the plug. But his hand had got wet. He licked it. And to
his surprise the water burned his tongue.

"*Hoo!*" he cried. "A new kind of water! Ah, I know what I will do. I will decree that whoever can drink this barrel of a new kind of water will be allowed to marry my daughter."

King Gorilla sent his servant, the totopodie bird, to carry this challenge to likely prospects. The king told her to look for men who were big and strong and brave.

Totopodie flew off at once. She said to herself, "Elephant is big and strong and brave." So she went to him and said, "I have a word for you."

"Speak," said Elephant. "I will listen."

Totopodie said:

"Drink a whole barrel of a new kind of water,
And marry King Gorilla's beautiful daughter."

Elephant laughed, *he, he, he.* "That will be easy for me!" he cried. "I drink half a barrel of water with every meal." And he followed the bird back to the royal village.

Now Princess Gorilla was watching from the doorway of her hut. She saw Elephant come in. "Oh, no!" she whispered. "*Oh, no!*"

As he went to the barrel Elephant said to King Gorilla, who was sitting nearby, "*Puh!* I can drink this in two gulps!"

Elephant thrust his trunk into the barrel. Then he withdrew
it, trumpeting and spraying the new kind of water all over the
king—EEEEEEEEEH! And he tramped off, *tobu, tobu, tobu.*

King Gorilla sputtered, *ih, ih, ih,* as he brushed the water off.
Princess Gorilla giggled with glee.

And the totopodie flew off to find another suitor. She said to herself, "Hippopotamus is big and strong and brave." So she went to him and said, "I have a word for you."

"Speak," said Hippopotamus. "I will listen."

Totopodie said:

> "Drink a whole barrel of a new kind of water,
> And marry King Gorilla's beautiful daughter."

"I *live* in the water," said Hippopotamus. "And that will be nothing for me."

"But this is a new kind of water," warned the bird.

Hippopotamus said, "New or old, hot or cold, water is water, I say." And he followed the bird back to the royal village.

Now Hog happened to be rooting nearby. He overheard all this. And he followed the bird and the hippopotamus.

Princess Gorilla saw the three come in at the gate. She sat on a stool to watch.

On his way to the barrel Hippopotamus said, "I *like* water. When I drink, the fish think the river is going dry!" He sank his big mouth into the barrel. Then he jerked it out, gagging, AAAAAAK! And he thundered off, *worom, worom*, back to the river to wash his mouth.

Princess Gorilla rocked on her stool with laughter.

Next Hog trotted up, *naka, naka, naka*. "Oh, King," he said, "let me try. I am accustomed to putting my nose into all sorts of dirty and smelly places."

The king gave his permission.

Carefully Hog dipped his snout into the barrel. Then he turned away in disgust and ran grunting, *nguh-uh-uh-uh,* all the way to the gate.

Princess Gorilla clapped her hands.

And the totopodie flew off to find another suitor. She said to herself, "Leopard is big and strong and brave." So she went to him and said, "I have a word for you."

"Speak," said Leopard. "I will listen."

Totopodie said:

> "Drink a whole barrel of a new kind of water,
> And marry King Gorilla's beautiful daughter."

N-nuf, sniffed Leopard. "We cats don't even like to get our paws wet. But I have heard of the beauty of the Princess Gorilla. For her I will do it, I will!" And he followed the bird back to the royal village.

Princess Gorilla saw Leopard come in.

And Leopard saw Princess Gorilla. He swaggered before her, switching his tail in anticipation. He put his forepaws on the rim of the barrel. The fumes made him sneeze, CHEH! He was embarrassed about that.

So he hastily gulped a big swallow of vinegar. It burned his throat. And he ran off panting, *huh-uh, huh-uh, huh-uh,* all the way to the gate.

Princess Gorilla danced with delight! No one was able to drink the new kind of water!

Just then a tiny talapoin ran to the king and bowed.

"Well, my little fellow," said the king, "what do you want?"

The little monkey replied, "Your Majesty, did you not say that anyone who drank the barrel of water might marry your daughter?"

King Gorilla chuckled, *hoo, hoo, hoo*. "That I did," he said.

"But, Your Majesty," continued Talapoin, "is it required that the barrel be emptied in one draft? May I not take a short rest in the grass between drinks?"

"I see no harm in that," said the king. "Just so the barrel is empty before the day darkens."

What the king did not know was that there were a hundred little monkeys, who all looked alike, hiding nearby in the grass.

Little Talapoin climbed up the barrel, took a sip of the new kind of water and leaped down into the grass. In a moment he apparently returned, took another sip, and jumped back. This was repeated over and over, but every time by a different monkey.

When each of the talapoins had had many turns, the barrel
was empty. Then they came popping out of the grass like grass-
hoppers. They swarmed about the king—*all* of them demanding
to marry the princess.

King Gorilla beat his chest, *hun, hun, hun!* The barrel was empty. He had to keep his word. But *how?*

Suddenly Leopard, who had been hiding near the gate, came bounding up, shouting, "You miserable little *cheaters*! Take that, and that!" And he batted the little monkeys left and right.

Then, PWIM! They scattered into the nearest trees and they never came back. Since that time, all talapoins live in the treetops. And, except in the mating season, male talapoins still travel in large groups. They remember that together they once did what Elephant, Hippopotamus, and Leopard could not do.

As for the beautiful Princess Gorilla—she married the handsome young male gorilla who sometimes played tag with her in the wawa trees.

And they lived happily ever after.